Ruby Gloom®

#2 Moon over Gloomsville

By Deirdre Black
Illustrated by Artful Doodlers

Grosset & Dunlap

GROSSET & DUNLAP
Published by the Penguin Group
Penguin Group (USA) Inc., 375 Hudson Street, New York, New York 10014, USA
Penguin Group (Canada), 90 Eglinton Avenue East, Suite 700, Toronto, Ontario M4P
2Y3, Canada (a division of Pearson Penguin Canada Inc.)
Penguin Books Ltd., 80 Strand, London WC2R 0RL, England
Penguin Group Ireland, 25 St. Stephen's Green, Dublin 2, Ireland
(a division of Penguin Books Ltd.)
Penguin Group (Australia), 250 Camberwell Road, Camberwell, Victoria 3124,
Australia (a division of Pearson Australia Group Pty. Ltd.)
Penguin Books India Pvt. Ltd., 11 Community Centre, Panchsheel Park,
New Delhi—110 017, India
Penguin Group (NZ), 67 Apollo Drive, Rosedale, North Shore 0632, New Zealand
(a division of Pearson New Zealand Ltd.)
Penguin Books (South Africa) (Pty.) Ltd., 24 Sturdee Avenue,
Rosebank, Johannesburg 2196, South Africa

Penguin Books Ltd., Registered Offices:
80 Strand, London WC2R 0RL, England

www.rubygloom.com

© 2008 Mighty Fine. Ruby Gloom is a registered trademark of Mighty Fine.
All rights reserved. Used under license by Penguin Young Readers Group.
Published by Grosset & Dunlap, a division of Penguin Young Readers Group,
345 Hudson Street, New York, New York 10014. GROSSET & DUNLAP
is a trademark of Penguin Group (USA) Inc. Printed in the U.S.A.

Library of Congress Control Number: 2007044117

ISBN 978-0-448-44673-8   10 9 8 7 6 5 4 3 2 1

Dear Friend,

Welcome to Gloomsville!

I live in a Victorian mansion with all of my friends. I can't wait for you to meet them. They mean the world to me.

There's Iris, a one-eyed girl who loves going on wild adventures; Skull Boy, who's always trying to figure out who he's descended from; Frank and Len, brothers who share a body and a love of loud music; Poe, a really smart crow; Misery, a girl with the worst luck in the world; Scaredy Bat, a little bat who's afraid of everything; Boo Boo, a ghost who isn't the least bit scary; and Doom Kitty, my best friend.

Sometimes I wonder what Gloomsville would be like if my friends and I were different. What if Iris didn't seek adventure, or if Misery's luck took a turn for the better? Have you ever wondered what it would be like to be different for the day?

Turn the page to find out what happened to my friends and me when we went camping during a lunar eclipse. Things got pretty strange, but luckily, good friends like mine are there for one another (especially in unfamiliar territory).

Your friend,

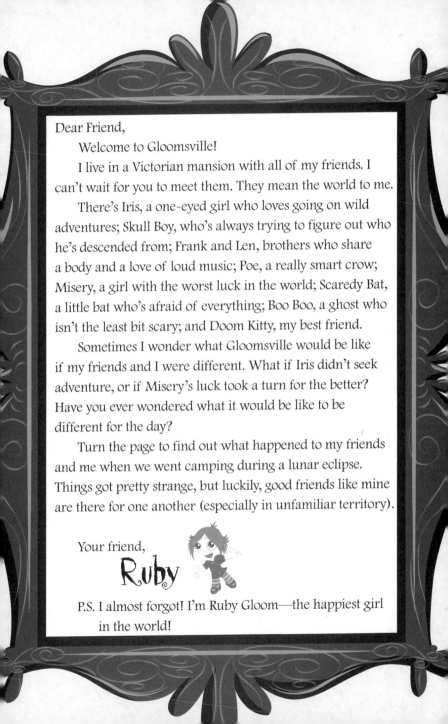

Ruby

P.S. I almost forgot! I'm Ruby Gloom—the happiest girl in the world!

Chapter One

"Take the road
less traveled and you'll find
more surprises."

It was a beautifully rainy night in Gloomsville. The full moon shone brightly on an old Victorian mansion on the edge of town. Everyone inside was relaxing or getting ready for bed. Ruby Gloom was brushing her red hair in front of her bedroom mirror. She smiled as she set down the brush. Everything made Ruby happy—after all, she was the happiest girl in the

world! Doom Kitty, Ruby's cat and best friend, jumped gracefully up onto Ruby's vanity and yawned. She was ready for bed, too.

Down in the basement, Misery was rearranging her collection of antique dolls. Her drab, purple dress dragged along the ground as she moved the dolls from one rickety shelf to another. Just then, she caught her toe in a hole in the floor and fell forward. The porcelain doll she was carrying smashed as it hit the ground. She sighed.

"Gee. What a surprise," she said in her low, gravelly voice. Misery seemed to be the unluckiest person in the world. In fact, every single person in Misery's family tree had terrible luck. As Misery began cleaning up the mess, she heard music drifting through the night air.

The music was coming from the garage, where Frank and Len were busy tuning their guitars. Frank and Len were two brothers who shared a body. But sometimes two heads are better than one, and Frank and Len made the perfect team. Both brothers loved wearing punk-rock clothes and playing extremely loud music.

Down in the Great Hall, Scaredy Bat was searching for the perfect, not-too-frightening spot to relax for a little while before going to bed. Lightning flashed outside and the little bat shuffled nervously away from the window. Scaredy was afraid of thunderstorms, the dark, and even flying—despite being a bat. In fact, Scaredy was pretty much scared of everything.

Just then, Scaredy felt a cool breeze tickle the back of his neck. He shrieked and dived behind a wingback chair. Laughter echoed through the room. Scaredy peeked over the back of the chair to see Boo Boo chuckling at him.

Boo Boo was the mansion's resident ghost-in-training. He was trying to learn to be terrifying,

but, with his chubby cheeks and mischievous smile, he was too cute to be scary. The only person he ever managed to frighten was Scaredy Bat, and that wasn't that much of a challenge.

"Boo Boo," Scaredy said as he laughed nervously, "you have gotten me once again. You are quite frightening." The two friends chuckled and set off toward Scaredy's room.

Nearby, in the library, Skull Boy and Iris were sitting at a large table. A chessboard was laid out between them and Skull Boy was deciding on his next move. He had thought that he might be related to Wilhelm Steinitz, the first official

World Chess Champion, so now he was trying to learn how to play. Skull Boy's family tree was a mystery to him, and he spent much of his time trying to figure out who his relatives might be.

Iris jiggled her foot restlessly under the table as her one large eye darted around the room. Chess wasn't really her game. She liked going on action-filled adventures and had trouble sitting still. She shifted in her seat and knocked the table hard with her foot. The chessboard went flying into the air, scattering white and black pieces across the floor.

"Whoops!" Iris said sheepishly.

"That's okay," Skull Boy reassured her. "I don't think I'm very good at chess after all. We've been playing all night and I haven't won a single game. Maybe I'm not descended from a chess master."

"I don't think chess is all that great, anyway," said Iris. "It would be much cooler if you were descended from someone like Meriwether Lewis or William Clark. You know, great adventurers or explorers?"

"I'd love a good adventure," Skull Boy exclaimed. "Maybe I am related to them. I'll have to look into it tomorrow." And, with that, he and Iris headed off to their respective rooms, chatting about explorers.

Meanwhile, high above the mansion, Poe sat staring up at the full moon through his window. Poe was a very intelligent crow who lived with his brothers, Edgar and Allen, in a cozy coop. He claimed that they were descended from the great writer Edgar Allan Poe's pet bird, Paco. Poe loved reading and writing poetry, especially on inspirational nights like the one they were having.

"What a lovely moon tonight," he muttered. "I really should compose an ode . . ."

He hopped up and began pacing in his den. "Oh, full moon," he said. "'Tis for you I swoon . . ."

As he approached his typewriter, Poe noticed his calendar hanging overhead. He stopped short. A big red *X* had been marked on the next day.

"Now why did I . . . Oh no!" Poe gasped. "Edgar! Allen!" he called as he began pecking away at his typewriter.

His brothers entered and stood silently on either side of Poe as he typed wildly.

"Something quite terrible is about to happen," Poe said finally. "It is urgent that we notify everyone at once. Here," he continued, dumping several freshly typed scrolls into his brothers' arms. "I will hold a lecture in the Great Hall at noon tomorrow. Please make sure that everyone is properly invited."

Edgar and Allen stood beside the desk and exchanged a glance.

"Thank you, dear brothers," Poe said, scuttling away. "I must prepare for my lecture."

Edgar and Allen exchanged another glance, then walked somberly from the chamber.

"It's bedtime, Doom Kitty," Ruby Gloom said as she slipped under her covers and pulled on her sleeping mask. "Tomorrow we start rehearsing for a new play I want to put on, *Doom Kitty on a Hot Tin Roof.*"

Knock. Knock.

"Who could that be, Doom?" Ruby said with a yawn. Doom Kitty hardly stirred in her bed. Her tail only lazily formed a question mark.

"It's so late," Ruby said, pulling up her mask and rubbing her eyes. But she dropped her feet to the floor and opened the door. Two huge shadowy figures looked down at her. Lightning struck with a great crash, and long shadows stretched into Ruby's room.

"Oh, hi, Edgar and Allen," Ruby said with a smile. "What's going on?"

Edgar held out a parchment scroll.

"Thanks . . . ?" Ruby said, taking the scroll, and Edgar and Allen walked off.

"Looks like mail, Doom," Ruby said, sitting on the edge of her bed. Doom Kitty flicked off her own sleeping mask with her tail and hopped

onto Ruby's bed. She peeked around her best
friend to get a closer look at the letter.

"Oh, it's from Poe," Ruby said. Then she
read out loud, "'To all occupants: It is with
great trepidation that I must call this emergency
meeting. Please gather at the Great Hall fireplace
at noon tomorrow. This matter is of the utmost
urgency!'"

"Hmm," Ruby said when she'd finished reading. "Wonder what could be so important . . . I guess we'll find out tomorrow." Then she put the scroll on her bedside table and climbed back under the covers, and she and Doom fell asleep to the musical sounds of crashing thunder.

Down the hall, wide awake and shaking quietly, Scaredy Bat lay curled up on his hammock beneath the biggest window in the house. Moonlight bathed the floor, and lightning cracked and boomed outside.

"Oh dear," Scaredy stammered. "I am not at all fond of darkness," he added. "But I'd rather have darkness than li—" *Crash! Boom!* "Lightning!"

Scaredy tucked his head under his wing and shook even more. For a few moments, no lightning cracked, and Scaredy began to relax.

"Perhaps I will be able to get some sleep," he said to himself with a sigh, and he closed his eyes and smiled peacefully.

CRRAAAACCKK!

Scaredy's eyes shot open as the hallway lit up like a ten-thousand-watt bulb. "Ahh!" he screamed. Before him were two towering shadows. "Please do not harm me!" he cried.

One of the figures raised his arm, and he was holding something in his hand.

"Oh dear," Scaredy muttered. "Ruby? Iris? . . . Anybody?" He squeezed his eyes tight, bracing himself. "Help!" he shrieked.

But after several uneventful moments, he dared to open one eye. The shadowy figures were gone. On the floor where the figures had been was a scroll.

"What is this?" he said, picking it up and unrolling it. "Poe is calling a meeting for tomorrow at noon?"

"Oh dear." Scaredy rolled the paper back up. "This doesn't sound like good news."

Edgar and Allen walked cautiously down the stairs. The walls along the basement steps were cracked. The pictures on the walls had fallen a long time ago, and they lay broken on the floor. The stairs themselves were uneven, and with every step, the brothers thought they might fall.

The basement was always like this. It was, of course, where Misery's room was. Misery's family had a history of bad things happening around them—and Misery herself was no exception.

Finally Edgar and Allen reached the bottom of the steps and came to Misery's door. Each crow took a deep breath, then let out a great sigh. Together, they knocked.

To their surprise, the door did not collapse at their feet. They both smiled and relaxed. Then: "Come in!" came a voice from inside. It shook the whole basement.

When the ceiling began to crumble and the floor began to quake, Edgar opened the door just wide enough to toss the scroll inside. Then, with their delivery made, the brothers scurried off down the crumbling hall to the safety of a more predictable part of the mansion.

As the scroll landed at Misery's feet, her shoulders sagged. "Oops," she said, then scooped up the scroll and glided back to bed.

Edgar and Allen walked slowly down the

hall to their chambers. They had made several deliveries that night—to Ruby Gloom and Doom Kitty; to Misery and Scaredy Bat; to Skull Boy, Iris, and even the deafening musical duo, Frank and Len, in the garage. But they still had one scroll left.

The last scroll was for the member of the household that was hardest to find: Boo Boo.

Usually the little ghost was hiding in a closet, or under some stairs, or behind a door, just waiting to jump out and shout a hearty "Boo!"—usually at Scaredy Bat. He kept track of his scares in a little notebook he carried with him everywhere. After all, it's important for a ghost—no matter how cute he is—to have a record of how frightening he can be.

Soon Edgar and Allen reached the door to their tower. Edgar reached for the door, and suddenly, just as the door creaked open: "Boo!"

It was Boo Boo. He floated before them,

giggling and pointing at the brothers. "I scared you, right?" he said, then laughed some more.

The brothers looked at each other, and then Edgar deposited a scroll right into Boo Boo's mouth. They stepped into the tower chamber and closed the door behind them.

"Hey!" Boo Boo called after them, pulling

the scroll from his mouth. After a moment he simply shrugged, pulled out his notepad, and scribbled down, "Midnight, Friday: Scared Edgar and Allen on tower steps."

Chapter Two

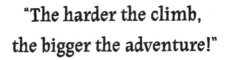

"The harder the climb,
the bigger the adventure!"

"Hi, gang!" Skull Boy said with a wave as he walked into the Great Hall the next day.

Ruby Gloom was already seated in one of the velvet chairs beside the fire. Doom Kitty was perched high above her head on the back of the chair.

"Hi, Skull Boy!" Ruby said with a smile. "Does anyone know what this meeting is about?"

Misery, sitting on the seat opposite Ruby's, shook her head.

Iris, who was pacing before the fire, replied,

"I have no idea, Ruby, but it better be important! Skull Boy and I were planning on climbing Mount Morose today."

"Just like Lewis and Clark!" Skull Boy added.

"I'd like to come, too," Misery said slowly. "My great-great-great-grandmother climbed Mount Morose . . . back when it was still known as Happiness Hill."

Iris and Ruby exchanged a knowing look.

"I can't imagine why they changed the name," Misery added, without the slightest bit of irony.

"We could all go!" Ruby exclaimed.

At that moment, Frank and Len stepped into the hall. "We're here!" Len announced.

"The meeting can begin!" added Frank, and the brothers capped off their entrance with a ripping guitar solo.

"Not quite yet," Ruby said. "Poe isn't here."

"So you guys got this weird invite, too?" said Len, holding up the scroll from Poe.

"Yup," said Iris. "We all did!"

"Maybe Poe has a new opera he wants to debut," suggested Skull Boy.

"Or another poem," suggested Misery with a sigh.

Just then, the big clock began to chime. The gang sat silently by the fire, listening to the twelve gongs. The only other sound was from Scaredy Bat's chattering teeth.

After the final gong, Edgar and Allen strode down the grand steps and into the Great Hall.

"Greetings," Poe announced gravely as he appeared between his brothers. He hopped over to the fireplace and then took off his hat.

The crow then turned to face the fire, deep in thought. "Thank you all for coming, but I'm afraid I have some terrible news."

"What's going on, Poe?" Ruby asked.

"Yeah," Misery drawled. "We were planning to climb Mount Morose today."

"Ahem!" Poe interjected. "I am sorry to spoil your fun, but you shall have to cancel your

climb—at least until tomorrow. It would be far too dangerous to attempt such a thing today."

The gang muttered to one another, confused.

Poe continued, "From now until sunrise tomorrow,

you'll all have to stay right here: inside the mansion."

"What?" Iris said, jumping to her feet. "Stay inside all day and night?"

"Come on, Poe, old pal," Skull Boy said, getting to his feet and throwing his bony arm around Poe. "Are you upset you weren't invited? You can go, too!"

"I can? Oh, how wonderful! A climb up Mount—" Poe suddenly stopped and shook his head. "That's not it at all! According to my observations and lengthy research, tonight a *lunar eclipse* will come to Gloomsville!"

Everyone gasped.

"A lunar eclipse?" Ruby exclaimed.

"Over Gloomsville?" Misery added.

"Oh my," Scaredy stuttered. "That does not sound like something I would particularly like to see."

The group was silent for a few moments.

Finally Len broke the silence. "Um, what's a lunar eclipse?" he asked.

"I know all about lunar eclipses," Skull Boy replied, pulling a rolled-up poster from his pocket. He unrolled the poster and held it in front of the others. "I have a family chart here that shows I am descended from several great astronomers, including the great Nicolaus Copernicus!"

Skull Boy took Poe's spot at the front of the group and cleared his throat. "A lunar eclipse," he explained, "is when the moon disappears from the sky."

"Oh dear!" Scaredy exclaimed, diving into Poe's cloak for cover. "The moon will . . . d-d-disappear?"

"Coooool," Len said. Misery oohed, and Ruby and Iris ahhed.

"Yes," Poe replied, picking up a fire poker and stabbing at the coals. Sparks flew and the flames cracked. "The moon disappears from the sky because it is covered by the Earth's shadow. But that is only half the problem."

Boo Boo, who was hovering over Misery's chair, said, "Half the problem?"

"Exactly," Poe went on, resuming his pacing in front of the fire. "For centuries, lunar eclipses have been known to have very strange effects on all who are unfortunate enough to see them."

"What kind of strange effects?" Ruby asked.

"Well, let's see," Poe replied. "For example, imagine that if I were to write a sonnet tonight . . . it might not be sublime!"

Iris blinked.

Skull Boy scratched his head.

Misery said slowly, "I don't get it."

"But, Poe," Ruby said, jumping to her feet. "That's not possible! You're a brilliant poet."

The others nodded vigorously and muttered in agreement.

"Exactly, Ruby," Poe said, tugging his lapel. "The eclipse would make me write horrible verse! And the eclipse will have the same effect on each of you!"

"But we don't write verse," Len said.

"I think," Frank said, shaking his head, "he means it would make, like, our tunes sound awful."

"Oh . . . oh no," Len stuttered. "Awful tunes?"

Poe nodded and clucked his tongue. "Now you see why this tragedy must be averted. We will all stay right here, out of the moonlight, in this very spot, until the sun comes up tomorrow and the eclipse is safely—"

"Poe, Poe, Poe . . ." Skull Boy said. "We're not afraid of a few silly little horrible tunes or bad poems—"

But Iris interrupted him. "Poe is right. We shouldn't climb Mount Morose today."

Ruby jumped to her feet. "Iris? That's not like you to cancel an outing!" she said, shocked.

"Aha!" Poe exclaimed, thrusting his finger in the air. "See? The effects of the eclipse have begun already!"

Iris laughed. "No, Poe," she said. "I don't want to *cancel* the climb because of the eclipse. I just want to *change* the climb to an overnight campout instead! This sounds like a perfect adventure!"

Ruby clapped and cheered. "That's perfect! We'll have a wonderful view of the eclipse from up there."

Len yelled, "Woo!" and the brothers delivered another awesome guitar solo.

Misery said, "Perfect. Great-Great-Grandmother Maelstrom would be so proud."

"What?" Poe said, trying to get between Iris and the others. "Haven't you been listening to me?"

"Yup," Iris replied as she left the Great Hall. "It's adventure time. I better get the camping gear packed."

"Sure, we listened," Ruby added. "It'll be fun to have our personalities change when that eclipse happens."

"Yeah, Poe," said Len. "Being the same all the time gets boring!"

"I'll go and get my telescope!" Skull Boy said as he took off up the stairs. "If only the great Copernicus could be here to see me now!"

"I'll go get my tent and sleeping bag,"

Ruby said. "Come on, Doom Kitty! We're going camping!"

Doom Kitty gracefully dropped from the top of the chair where she'd been perched and followed Ruby up the grand staircase to Ruby's room.

"Everyone, please!" Poe called as the others left the Great Hall to get ready for their camping trip. "I must warn you all again not to go outside tonight!"

"Oh, please listen to him!" Scaredy muttered from under Poe's cloak, where he'd been hiding. He poked his head out. "Well," he continued, "I will most certainly stay here with you, Poe. Nothing could convince me to camp overnight on Mou—Mount Morose!"

"Boo!"

"Aah!" Scaredy Bat shrieked, and he bolted up the steps to join the others who were getting ready. "Wait for me! Do not leave me here!"

Boo Boo giggled as the bat fled the hall. "Twelve thirty, Saturday afternoon," he said, scribbling in his notepad. "Frightened Scaredy Bat in the Great Hall. Ha ha!"

Chapter Three

"When traveling, don't forget
to bring along the most
important thing—friends."

That evening, the gang started the long hike
to the camping spot at the top of Mount Morose.
The full moon hung low over Gloomsville. Its
eyes followed the gang happily as they headed
up the mountain.

"Huh. The moon looks the same as always to
me," said Ruby.

"Yes," said Scaredy Bat with a smile. "A normal, bright, not-dangerous, wonderful, eclipse-free moon."

Doom Kitty pranced at Ruby's side, eyeing Frank and Len. The brothers were struggling with a teetering load of equipment as they walked up the trail.

"Do we have everything, Frank?" Len asked his brother.

"I think so, Len," Frank replied. "Let's see . . . we've got our guitars."

"Check!" said Len.

"Amps?" asked Frank.

"Check!" Len said.

"Recording equipment?" added Frank.

"And check!" said Len with a smile.

"Why did you guys bring all that to go camping?" Ruby asked.

"Ruby, Ruby, Ruby," said Frank. "How would it be if two great musicians like us didn't have our gear during such an inspirational night?"

"Right on!" agreed Len.

Iris shook her head. "Didn't you guys bring any *camping* equipment?" she cried.

Len rolled his eyes. "Of course we did. See?" he said, and nodded to a camping lantern that sat tottering atop the stack of amps and guitars in his arms.

Suddenly, Frank and Len stumbled. "Whoops!" Len said, and the lantern tipped, flipped, and fell from the top of the stack.

Doom Kitty sprung ahead and snatched the lantern with her tail just before it crashed to the ground. The little flame never even went out.

"Good catch, Doom," said Ruby, patting the cat on the head. "You're always so graceful. And we're going to need that lantern soon!"

Skull Boy nodded. "Yup," he said. "Soon the moon will be gone completely! We'll need the lantern to see."

"I hope something happens soon," said Iris. "Because so far, I don't feel any different!"

Misery nodded. "Me either," she said sadly. As she spoke, a bolt of lightning shot from the clear night sky and hit a tree on the side of the path.

"Well," said Ruby, "at least that lightning didn't hit you! Maybe you *have* changed!"

But just as she said it, the highest branch on the tree gave a loud crack, broke off from the trunk, and came speeding down to the ground, clobbering Misery.

"Ouch," Misery said as Ruby helped her get to her feet.

"Oh . . . well," Ruby said. "I guess I spoke too soon."

They continued their hike up the mountain.

Suddenly Skull Boy stopped and pointed up at the sky. "Look, everyone, it's starting!" Sure enough, the moon was slowly being covered in shadow.

"It's awfully sad that the moon has to disappear like that," Ruby commented to no one

in particular as they
started walking again.
Doom Kitty moved to
the front of the line,
holding the lantern up
high with her tail to
light the way.

"I'm getting tired,"
Iris said. "Aren't we
there yet?"

Scaredy Bat walked
faster and caught up to Doom Kitty at the front
of the group. "It is not far now, Iris!"

Scaredy Bat was right, and in a few more
minutes they'd reached the campsite. The moon
had almost completely vanished from sight. "See
that red glow up there?" Len said, pointing to
where the moon had been. "That's all that's left
of the moon."

Frank nodded. "That's right, Len. It's known

as a total eclipse of the moon!"

The gang all looked up at the red glow in the night sky. "Oh, big deal about some dumb eclipse," Skull Boy said suddenly. "Who cares about astronomy? Not me!"

"I couldn't agree more," said Iris with a great sigh. She continued to whine. "And my feet hurt from all this walking. And I'm all sweaty. When do we get to sleep?"

"Iris doesn't seem to be enjoying this adventure very much," Frank whispered to Len.

"You're right, and that isn't like her at all. Maybe she's just a little tired," Len answered.

Iris took off her pack and started to set up her tent, but the ropes got tangled, the tarp got twisted, and the poles kept falling on her head. Soon the tent was a heap on the ground.

Meanwhile, Misery walked around the campsite, carrying her own tent and giggling. "This eclipse is hilarious," she said, smiling.

"Poe is so silly," she added with a chuckle. "Nothing has even happened." Suddenly, Misery tripped. The folded-up tent she had been carrying went flying into the air.

"Oops," she said, and laughed. But as she got to her feet, the tent came falling back toward the campsite. Misery and the others watched as it fell back down and landed, somehow perfectly pitched and ready for bedtime.

Iris's mouth dropped open and she looked at her own tent, which was still in a heap at her feet. She called to Misery, "Will you pitch my tent, too? It's too hard for me."

"Whoa," said Len. "That was *lucky*."

"My thoughts exactly," agreed Frank. He rubbed his chin, deep in thought, and then whispered, "You know, Misery is usually the most unlucky person in the world. And Iris never thinks anything is too difficult."

"Hmm . . . perhaps the eclipse really is affecting our personalities," Len said, his voice low.

"I think you might be right," Frank agreed. "But we should probably observe their behavior for a while to make certain."

"Quite right," Len replied. "We must have conclusive evidence before we present our findings to everyone."

Ruby kicked the dirt and grumbled. "Dumb eclipse. There's nothing special about it at all!"

Scaredy Bat hopped up beside his friends. "Oh, the eclipse is okay," he said. "But what would be much more fun is bungee jumping off that cliff over there." He started walking toward a cliff near the campsite.

"Have fun, Scaredy," Frank called after him. "That's very *brave* of you!"

Len added, "Yes, *quite* brave." He winked at his brother. "Meanwhile, we're going to stay here to work out the mathematical properties of your velocity as you jump off the cliff and fall toward the earth."

"Well," said Ruby as she sat on the ground, feeling sad. Doom Kitty curled up next to her and closed her eyes. "I guess this is going to be a boring night after all, huh, Doom?"

Just then, a toad hopped by. Doom's eyes popped open, and she slowly crawled after it

toward a nearby muddy creek. But as she stalked it, a twig cracked under her paws, and soon she tripped over a root and fell right on her face. The toad scampered off quickly.

Ruby, though, didn't see Doom leave or stumble on the root. She was too busy watching as Iris followed Scaredy Bat. "Scaredy Bat," Iris called after him timidly. "I don't know if that's a good idea . . ."

"Please do not worry, Iris," Scaredy Bat said as he tied a big elastic band to his waist. He was preparing to go bungee jumping. "I live for danger!"

Ruby felt tears form in her eyes as she watched her friends. "This is so saaaad," she said, and she reached for Doom to pet her.

But Doom wasn't at her side. "Doom?" said Ruby.

No reply.

"Doom Kitty?" Ruby called out as a tear slid

down her cheek. She waited a few moments, but Doom didn't answer her call.

"Scaredy Bat! Iris!" Ruby yelled as she got to her feet. "Come back! Doom Kitty's gone!"

Chapter Four

"Be careful what you wish
for; it may come true."

"Do not fear," Scaredy Bat said as he
comforted Ruby. "I am certain we will find
Doom Kitty in no time at all."

Ruby sobbed and blew her nose with a great
honk. "Thanks"— *sniff* —"Scaredy, but it's
hopeless! Doom is gone
forever."

Misery, who
had finished setting
up all the tents,
giggled as she sat
next to Iris. "We'll

find Doom Kitty," Misery said. "See? There's a paw print over there by the creek," she added, pointing to a muddy spot a few feet away.

Skull Boy walked over to the mud and leaned over the paw print. "How did you spot that?" Skull Boy said.

Misery shrugged. "Just lucky, I guess," she said.

Frank and Len looked up from their complicated math formula and exchanged a glance. "Lucky, huh?" Len muttered. The brothers nodded. Len pulled out a small journal and made a note.

"I wish I could help," Skull Boy replied. "But I don't think I'd be any good at tracking or detective work . . ."

Ruby squinted through her tears at Skull Boy. "Didn't you tell us that you thought you had a great-uncle who was a detective?"

Skull Boy shrugged and his shoulders sagged.

"Maybe, but I doubt that would have any effect on my talents," he said.

Frank and Len walked over and examined the paw print closely. "Doom Kitty was here, all right," Frank said, stroking his chin.

"Indeed," his brother added. "And she headed north. That way!" Len pointed toward the peak of Mount Morose.

"Onward!" Scaredy Bat announced, with his wings on his hips. "We must march to the peak to find Doom Kitty."

"What's the use?" Ruby said, grumpily getting to her feet.

"Ugh," Iris said. "More walking? No thanks. I'll wait here."

"Come on, Iris," Ruby sniffed. She grabbed her friend by the arm to help her to her feet. "I'm sure we won't find her, but at least we won't be in this awful place anymore."

The gang followed Scaredy north, toward

the craggy peak of Mount Morose. "This way! There is nothing to fear!" he called back to them as he marched ahead.

"I . . . I don't like this," Iris said, hanging back. The trail was overgrown and dark. Strange noises came from the woods on either side as they walked. "What was that?!" Iris cried, grabbing Skull Boy.

"How would I know?" Skull Boy replied. "Do I look like a zoologist to you?"

"Didn't you once say you might be related to Jane Goodall, the famous zoologist who was known for living in the jungle with wild animals?" Iris asked.

Skull Boy shrugged. "Don't know. Don't care."

"We're in for it," Ruby said, wiping tears from her eyes. "I'll never see Doom Kitty again!"

Another noise came from the woods—this time a loud crash.

"Aah!" Iris screamed, and she jumped in the air, landing in Misery's arms.

"Nice catch, Misery," Ruby said with a sniffle. "That was pretty lucky."

"Yeah," Misery said. "My luck sure is good today."

Frank and Len both smiled and nodded at each other. Now they were certain that the eclipse was affecting everyone's personalities. "It is time we let you all in on something. My brother and I have developed a hypothesis!" Frank exclaimed.

"We have indeed!" Len said. "This is all the effect of the eclipse!"

"What"—*sniff*—"effect?" Ruby asked, frowning.

"Yes," Scaredy Bat bellowed, hopping over. "Tell me where these effects are, and I will rescue us all!"

"Don't you guys see?" replied Frank. "Misery is having the best luck of her life . . ."

"That's true," said Misery.

"And Iris keeps complaining about how hard and scary everything is, but she's usually the most adventurous one out of all of us," added Len. "And Scaredy Bat is behaving like a hero, but he is usually scared of everything!"

"Of course," Len finished, "Skull Boy isn't interested in anything, no matter what kind of family history there might be! Plus Ruby is feeling hopeless, and we all know she's the happiest girl in the world."

Len scratched his head. "The only thing puzzling me," he said, "is what effect has it had on *us*?"

Frank thought for a second. "Len," he said,

"it's so obvious: We've switched heights. You're now one millimeter taller than me."

Just then, a loud crash came from the woods just off the path.

"Aah!" Iris shouted, hiding behind Frank and Len.

"I think something is following us!" said Scaredy Bat, and he ran to the edge of the trees. "How exciting!" he added in a whisper.

"Let's keep moving," Iris said, eager to get away from whatever was lurking in the woods.

The friends continued on, Scaredy Bat in the lead, marching valiantly, and Iris at the back, huddling behind the others. "Guys," Iris said, "maybe we should head back to camp. This doesn't seem safe."

A crash came from the woods to their right.

"And something is *definitely* following us!" Iris added, grabbing Skull Boy's arm.

"There is nothing to fear!" called Scaredy Bat

from the front of the group. "Whatever it is that is following us, it will have to go through me!"

Suddenly, something burst from the bushes. It bounded past the gang, flinging mud everywhere in its wake.

"Aaah!" Iris screamed.

Frank and Len ducked as the thing flipped and bounced over their heads. Len reached up to try to grab it.

Ruby could just make out something red on a slimy, brown body. Then, just as quickly, it went crashing noisily into the woods on the other side of the trail.

"Did you get a sample, Len?" Frank asked.

Len squinted at his fingertips. "I think so, Frank," he replied. His fingertip was coated in a thick brown goop.

"What—what was that?!" Iris said with a whimper, grabbing Misery's arm.

"It looked like some kind of monster," Frank suggested.

"Doom Kitty doesn't stand a chance with a monster around," Ruby sobbed.

"From its dirty skin and brown color, and this sample of mud I managed to collect, I have deduced that it lives in a muddy swamp," said Len.

"I—I think there's a muddy swamp that way," said Iris, pointing off the trail. "I hiked up here one time . . . though I can't imagine why." With that, she plopped down and sat right on the trail.

"Well," said Misery, "that's the direction the monster came from. And that's also the direction of our camp. Maybe the *monster* has seen Doom Kitty?"

"There is only one way to find out!" Scaredy announced. "We must catch the swamp monster of Mount Morose!"

He thrust his fist into the air and his wings flapped behind him like a mighty cape. He was a heroic sight to behold. In fact, Frank and Len applauded.

"Oh no!" Iris said suddenly.

"What is it now?" Ruby said, beginning to weep again. "Something totally *sad*?"

"Yes, something sad." Iris sighed as she got to her feet. "This sounds like it means more *walking*."

Chapter Five

"Together, friends
can survive anything—
even rapids!"

"Okay, everyone," whispered Frank. "Stay completely quiet."

The gang was huddled in the bushes along the muddy swamp Iris had mentioned.

"My pleasure," said Iris. "Just let me know when it's time for f-f-*fleeing!*"

"If my hypothesis is correct," said Len quietly, "then that swamp monster will be back any moment."

"And then," said Scaredy Bat, a little too loudly, "we shall catch the beast!"

"Shhh!" said the others.

"We're not trying to catch the swamp monster," said Ruby through a crying hiccup. Her cheeks were stained with tears. "We're just going to ask if it's seen *Dooo-ooo-oom*!" And she began to wail with sadness.

Misery, meanwhile, sat beside her, giggling uncontrollably. "Whoa, guys," she said through her laughter. Something hard and lumpy was digging into her back. "I think I'm sitting on something."

Misery stood up and found she'd been sitting on a large butterfly net. "Hee hee!" she said with

glee, and picked up the net. "Someone must have lost this. What luck! Maybe we can use this to . . ."

"Misery," interrupted Frank, "standing up so everyone can see you defeats the purpose of hiding in this bush for our stakeout!"

"Oh!" Misery suddenly said with a snort. She jumped up and down with glee. "There it is!" Still standing, she pointed over the bushes toward the muddy swamp.

"There what is?" asked Skull Boy. He squinted through the bushes into the dark of the swamp. "I don't see anything."

"It!" said Misery, giggling. "The swamp creature of Mount Morose!"

"Get down, Misery," said Frank urgently. "It'll see us! We are trying to surprise it!"

Misery chuckled. "Silly, it already *has* seen us. It's heading this way."

The others jumped to their feet.

"It *is* heading this way!" said Scaredy Bat. "Stay back, my friends. I shall protect you!"

Iris's mouth dropped open, but nothing came out. She only coughed and sputtered and shook.

"It's getting closer!" said Skull Boy. "What should we do?"

"Run!" shouted Iris, and she turned and took off through the woods.

"Wait a second," Ruby said quietly. "There's something about this monster . . ."

"It's moving pretty fast, Ruby," said Len. "Maybe Iris has the right idea!"

Even Misery wasn't laughing. "Yeah, Ruby," she said. "It doesn't look like it wants to be friends."

"It's speeding right at you, Ruby!" Skull Boy said. "I'm no monsterologist, but that doesn't seem friendly to me."

The monster, flinging mud everywhere, with big, green, leafy scales all over it, came bounding across the swamp toward Ruby.

"Guys," Ruby said, "I think it's . . ."

Scaredy Bat stepped between the charging monster and Ruby. "Run, Ruby!" he said. "I'll deal with this monster!"

At that very moment the swamp creature slipped, slid, and crashed right into Scaredy Bat. The monster and Scaredy fell into a heap on the bank of the muddy swamp.

"Unnhhh . . ." Scaredy said as he wobbily got to his feet. "Did I . . . did I win?" And he flopped face-first into the mud.

The swamp creature stood up, too. It hobbled toward the gang. Skull Boy, Frank, Len, and Misery stood behind Ruby, who crouched on the edge of the swamp, watching the monster approach.

Iris stood fifty yards back, watching. "The monster knocked out Scaredy Bat!" she called to her friends.

"And he was the bravest of us," Skull Boy pointed out. "We'd better run!"

"We have deduced that Skull Boy and Iris are correct," Frank announced. "Let's get out of here, Ruby!"

The monster stopped right in front of Ruby.

Skull Boy grabbed Ruby by the arm and pulled her along as the gang fled the swamp monster.

"Guys!" Ruby said through her tears. "I don't think we should be running away—"

Skull Boy was pulling Ruby along as they joined Iris and ran down the trail to the camp with Scaredy bringing up the rear. "It's gaining on us!" Iris shouted. "Run faster, everyone!"

Skull Boy, who was at the front of the group, came to a sudden stop. "Guys!" he said, and the others stopped, too. "The river bridge is out! We're trapped!"

Skull Boy was right: The river had washed over the bridge completely.

The gang stood on the bank of the river. They huddled together, feeling helpless as the swamp monster came racing toward them.

"Here it comes!" Frank shouted.

"We're dooooooomed!" Iris cried.

"Doomed?" Ruby muttered to herself.

At that moment the swamp monster leaped at Ruby.

"Look out!" Skull Boy yelled. But the monster missed Ruby completely, and sailed right over the gang, into the river behind them.

The friends stared at the water waiting for the monster to resurface. When it bobbed to the surface it managed to hoist itself onto a small rock sticking out of the water. Then it shook and shook, flinging mud and gunk into the river. When it had finished shaking itself free of all the gunk, everyone could see now that it wasn't a swamp monster after all—it was Doom Kitty!

"Doom!" Ruby said. "And she's stuck out there!" She sobbed and sobbed.

"We'll save her, Ruby," Skull Boy said. "Don't worry!"

"That's right, Ruby. We will rescue Doom Kitty," Scaredy said.

"And of course," said Len, "Frank and I
have a plan! We just need to borrow Misery's
butterfly net. We'll attach another stick to it and
then it should be long enough to scoop Doom
out of the river."

"Sure! I knew this would come in handy,"
Misery replied, handing the net to Frank
and Len.

Then the brothers ran to the edge of the trail
and picked up a long stick.

"Here!" Iris said, handing the brothers a ribbon. "You can use my hair tie to hold them together."

Together the gang lifted the net and held it out to Doom Kitty, who was struggling in the river.

"Jump in, Doom!" Ruby shouted through her sobs.

Doom just managed to leap off of the rock and into the net. The others swung it around, and soon Doom was safe on dry land—even if she happened to fall on her

face as soon as she jumped out of the net.

Ruby ran to Doom and threw her arms around the cat's wet neck. "I'm so glad you're all right, Doom!" she said, crying with relief this time.

The others dropped the net and gathered around Ruby and Doom Kitty.

"Aha!" Frank and Len said at the same time.

"Um, if you're going to say that the swamp monster is really Doom Kitty," said Misery with a chuckle, "we already knew that."

"Indeed," agreed Len.

"But," added Frank, "we have concluded also that the eclipse has made Doom Kitty maladroit and obtuse, rather than graceful and perspicacious."

The others blinked. "Huh?" they all said.

"She's clumsy and not as clever as usual right now," explained Frank.

"Ah," said the others.

"Well," Ruby said as Doom Kitty tried to lick the tears from her cheeks, "I guess we should get back to"—*sniff*—"camp. It's pretty late."

"Finally!" Iris said as she swatted at the air. "There are *bugs* here, you know! Blecch!"

Chapter Six

"To have a good friend,
you need to
be a good friend."

Soon, a roaring campfire crackled at the campsite. "Good idea to have some s'mores before bed, Skull Boy," Frank said. He held a marshmallow on a stick out over the fire.

Skull Boy looked over at Misery, who was skipping around the fire and giggling. "I'd rather be asleep," he admitted, "but Misery's hysterical laughter is keeping me up."

"That's so sad," Ruby said, sniffling. "I'm sorry, Skull Boy."

"I cannot sleep, either," said Scaredy Bat. "I am too excited for the next adventure!" He leaped to his feet and thrust out his chest. The others clapped, impressed with his heroism.

Misery stopped skipping long enough to grab a s'more. "As for me," she said with her mouth full, "how can I sleep? Hee hee! I can't stop laughing!" With that she fell to the floor, clutched her tummy, and burst into a fit of laughter.

"I wish I could sleep," said Iris. "I know that hike down the mountain is going to be really tough in the morning. If I don't sleep, it'll be *impossible*!"

"The scientific definition of sleep," said Len, "is a resting state during which one's eyes are closed and breathing is reduced to approximately eight breaths per minute."

"Elementary," added Frank. "Let's all practice breathing together. Maybe it will help us relax."

The brothers closed their eyes and began breathing slowly, counting each breath out loud. "One . . . two . . . three . . ."

Misery tried to join in, but that made her laugh even harder. She laughed so hard that she laughed herself right to exhaustion. Soon, she really was asleep.

And with Misery asleep and finally quiet, the others quickly fell off to sleep as well.

The next morning, the sun rose in a gloomy sky as the gang woke up, rubbing their eyes and yawning.

Without Ruby realizing it, a single raindrop splashed onto her cheek. "I think I'm crying," she said, wiping at it. "But I don't feel sad."

"You're not crying," said Skull Boy. "It's just raining a little."

"Oh," replied Ruby. She began to frown, but then she stopped. "Wait a second," she said gleefully. "I love the rain!"

Skull Boy nodded. "I don't know a thing about rain," he said. "Although . . . I think my grandfather may have been a weatherman." He jumped to his feet and unfolded a big map of Gloomsville. "Rain is moving in this morning from the

east," he said in a deep, weatherman-type voice. "We should expect showers through the afternoon!"

"Oh no," Iris replied, rolling over. "My socks are still wet from that dumb swamp, and now I have to take a long, tiring walk in the *rain* down Mount Mo—" But suddenly, she gasped. "A long walk in the rain down Mount Morose? That's awesome!" she said, and jumped for joy.

Misery had also woken up. She was still curled up on the ground near the fire. "I miss my bed of nails," she said, getting to her feet. At that very moment, an especially dark cloud floated over the campsite, and a bolt of lightning shot down. It struck Misery square on the head.

"Ow," she said. "Lucky me—back to normal."

"Looks like we all are," noted Ruby, and she pointed to Doom.

Her feline friend was gracefully balancing her dish on the end of her tail. It looked like Doom was ready for breakfast. Ruby poured Doom some milk while the others packed up all of their camping gear. When Doom finished eating she used her tail to point down the trail, letting the others know she was ready to go.

"It's good to have you back, Doom," Ruby said with a smile. "And it's good to be back to my usual self."

Meanwhile, Frank and Len gathered up all their gear. "Bummer," said Len. "We didn't get a chance to jam during the eclipse."

"Yeah, but it was still a cool trip," Frank said.

"Oh yeah," Len agreed. "And I got to be a millimeter taller than you for a whole night!"

"Dude!" Frank exclaimed. The brothers exchanged a high five and then joined the rest of the gang, their load of guitars, amps, recording equipment, and single glowing camping lantern at the very top, teetering in their arms.

"Whoops!" the brothers said together as Len's boot got caught on a rock. The lantern came flying toward the ground.

Doom Kitty shook her head at the brothers as she caught the lantern with her tail. It was going to be a long walk back to the mansion.

Chapter Seven

"Don't go changing—
unless you want to!"

"Finally!" said Poe as the gang walked into the Great Hall. "I trust you have seen the error of your ways by not heeding my advice yesterday."

He was standing near the huge fireplace, in the very spot where the gang had left him after his emergency meeting the day before. The fire was only a glowing pile of embers now. Edgar and Allen were standing beside Poe and leaning on each other, asleep. Poe himself looked like he had just woken up, having slept in his cape, monocle, and top hat.

"Poe," said Ruby, laughing, "have you been in the Great Hall this whole time?"

Doom Kitty shook her head in disbelief.

"I have," replied Poe. He yawned. "In fact, I have not even left this exact spot! Edgar, Allen, and I have been completely safe . . . if not entirely well rested. Er . . . but going out? Leaving this room?! Far, *far* too dangerous."

"You're not kidding," said Ruby as she settled into one of the high-backed chairs. "Last night was quite an adventure."

"I am not at all surprised," replied Poe, sitting in the other chair. "I shudder to think what awful things would have happened to me if I'd ventured from this spot last night. Just imagine it: horrible singing, terrible acting, tasteless poetry . . ."

He shook his head. "But, please," Poe said to the gang, "tell me what frightening events befell you last night."

"I was b-b-brave!" said Scaredy Bat with a shudder.

"And I was scared!" said Iris.

"And I kept having . . . good luck," added Misery with a sigh.

"I was so sad and Doom was horribly clumsy," Ruby giggled.

"And Frank and Len were brilliant!" added Skull Boy.

"But we're always brilliant," said Len, "so I guess the eclipse didn't affect *us*, but still . . ."

"Of course it did, Len," said Frank. "Remember? You were *taller* than me!"

"Mmhm, yes," muttered Poe. "But that all sounds rather *nice*, if you ask me. Scaredy Bat not being scared? Misery having good fortune! Iris not running headlong into danger all the time! Sounds simply wonderful. Come along, Edgar and Allen. I have an ode on the moon that needs finishing!" And with that, the crow

headed toward his
chambers. Edgar
and Allen, still half
asleep, plodded
along after their
brother.

Ruby laughed.
"He's right," she
said to her friends.
"It was pretty
wonderful to try
being different for
one night. But I'm glad to be myself again."

"Right," Iris agreed. "I always liked myself,
but before this lunar eclipse, I had no idea just
how *much*!"

"And how much I like my friends," added
Misery in her slow drawl, sitting down on the
empty high-backed chair. But, of course, it
collapsed beneath her, startling Scaredy Bat,

who sped off, tumbling into Skull Boy, who fell to the ground in a heap of bones, nearly covering Doom Kitty, who narrowly escaped by leaping onto Ruby's lap.

Ruby giggled and added, "Exactly—just the way we are!"

Dear Friend,

We certainly had a wild adventure on Mount Morose! Who would have thought that Doom Kitty could ever be mistaken for a swamp monster? Luckily, my friends and I were still there for one another, like always! Because friendship means sticking together, no matter what.

At first we were looking forward to being different for a night, but in the end we all realized that we like ourselves and one another—just the way we are. If Iris wasn't always seeking adventure and Scaredy didn't have fears to overcome, life in Gloomsville just wouldn't be the same!

Like I always say, you should always have an open mind and try everything at least once!

Your friend (no matter what!),

Ruby

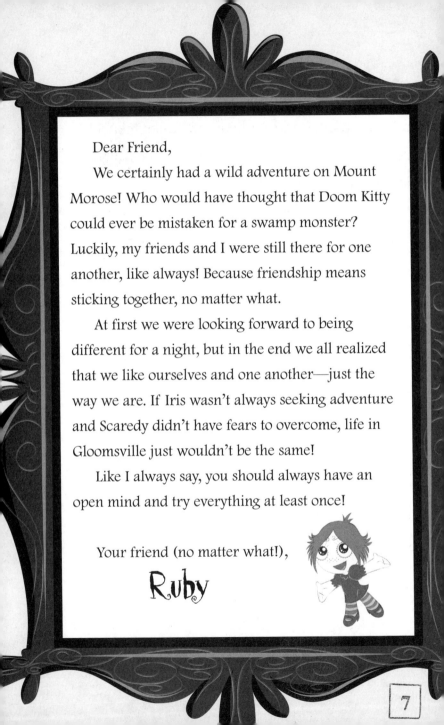